This book is for Shelby
—A.J.H.

ISBN 0-439-57947-3

Text copyright © 2003 by Anna Jane Hays.
Illustrations copyright © 2003 by Valeria Petrone. All rights reserved.
Published by Scholastic Inc., 557 Broadway, New York, NY 10012,
by arrangement with Random House Children's Books, a division of
Random House, Inc. SCHOLASTIC and associated logos are
trademarks and/or registered trademarks of Scholastic Inc.

12 11 10   20 21 22 23/0

Printed in the U.S.A.   40

First Scholastic printing, September 2003

The Pup Speaks Up

by Anna Jane Hays
illustrated by Valeria Petrone

SCHOLASTIC INC.
New York Toronto London Auckland Sydney
Mexico City New Delhi Hong Kong Buenos Aires

Bo has a new pal.

Happy day!

"Hello!" says Bo.

"What do you say?"

The pup just wags
his tail.

Bo and Pal
go for a walk.
"What do you say?"
Bo asks a duck.

"Quack," says the duck.

"Honk," goes a truck.

"What do you say?"

Bo asks a bee.

"Buzz," says the bee.

"Buzz like me."

"Tick tock,"
goes a clock.

"Chug, chug,"
goes a tug.

A train calls,
"Choo choo!"

A baby cries,

"Boo-hoo!"

A rooster crows,

"Cock-a-doodle-do!"

An owl hoots,

"Hoo hoo! Hoo hoo!"

"What do you say?"

Bo asks Pal.

Pal just runs

and chases his tail.

A chick says,
"Cheep."

"Baa, baa,"

says a sheep.

A happy pig says,
"Oink, oink, oink."

boink

boink

boink

A bouncy ball goes
boink, boink, boink.

"Ribbit," says a frog.

But not the dog.

"What do you say?"

Bo asks his pup.

This time Pal

just jumps up.

"Moo!" says a cow.

Look out now . . .

Here comes a cat!

It says,

"MEOW!"

The pup speaks up!
"BOW WOW WOW!"

Bo says, "WOW!"

Hooray!

What a happy day!